THIS BOOK

WAS DONATED

TO

BY

ON

BOOKS, GIFTS THAT KEEP ON GIVING

ITTY & BITTY

Two Miniature Horses

written by Nancy Carpenter Czerw

Nancy C. Czerw

illustrated by Dana Bauer

Dana Bauer

McWITTY PRESS, New York, NY

To the memory of my parents, William and Jane Carpenter —N.C.C.

For my mom and sister —D.B.

Designed by Kenneth B. Smith

Printed in Hong Kong
First edition
2005

ISBN 0-9755618-2-0

McWITTY PRESS
110 Riverside Dr., 1A
New York, NY 10024

I'm Itty. I'm **Bitty**.

We're itty, bitty minis–

Two Nosy NEIGHbors

Pint-size, just the right size,

For itty, bitty kiddies.

We run around barefoot,

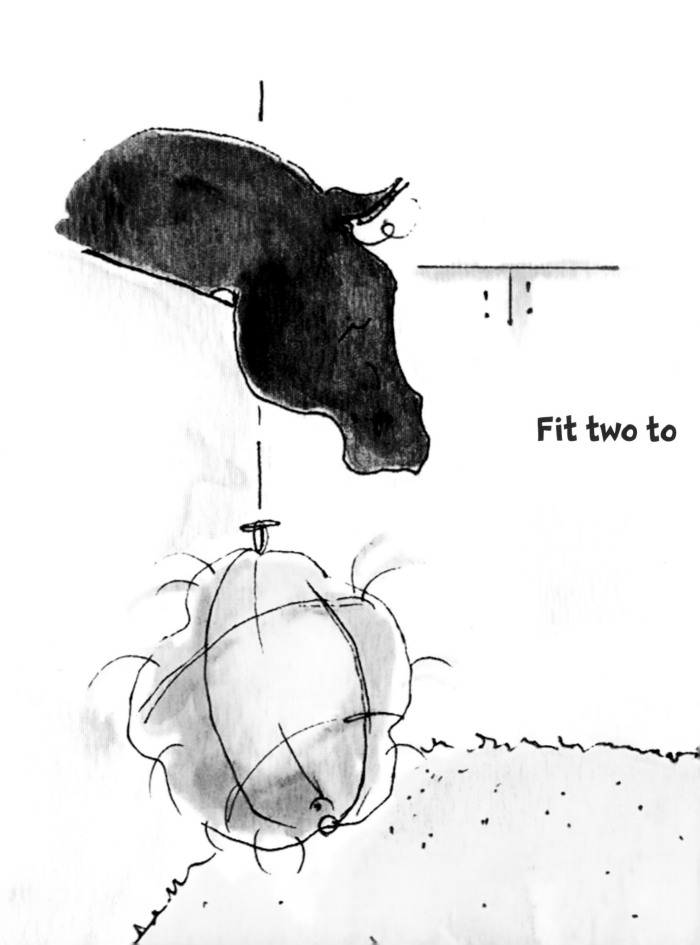

Fit two to

a stall,

And if you should ride us,

It's not far to fall.

Bitty is a ragamuffin–

Unkempt mane and too much stuffin'.

He thinks grooming's too much fuss.

He'd rather be a scruffy Gus!

Itty is a little vain.
Each day he combs his
tail and mane.

He wants to be a well-groomed man—
A dappled, polished, Dapper Dan!

Bitty is brave.

He stands on the dock.

Itty needs shade

And a 40 sun block.

When traveling distances not too far,

We'd really rather go in the car.

In the time
it takes
to hook up
the rig,

By the time the truck

And trailer are coupled,

We're in the car

With the seatbelts buckled.

It's hard to find a tiny bit

And bridle, small enough to fit

These tiny mouths
and tiny teeth,
And tiny tongues
and tiny cheeks.

We'll have to hunt

over hill and dale

To find a mini-martingale!

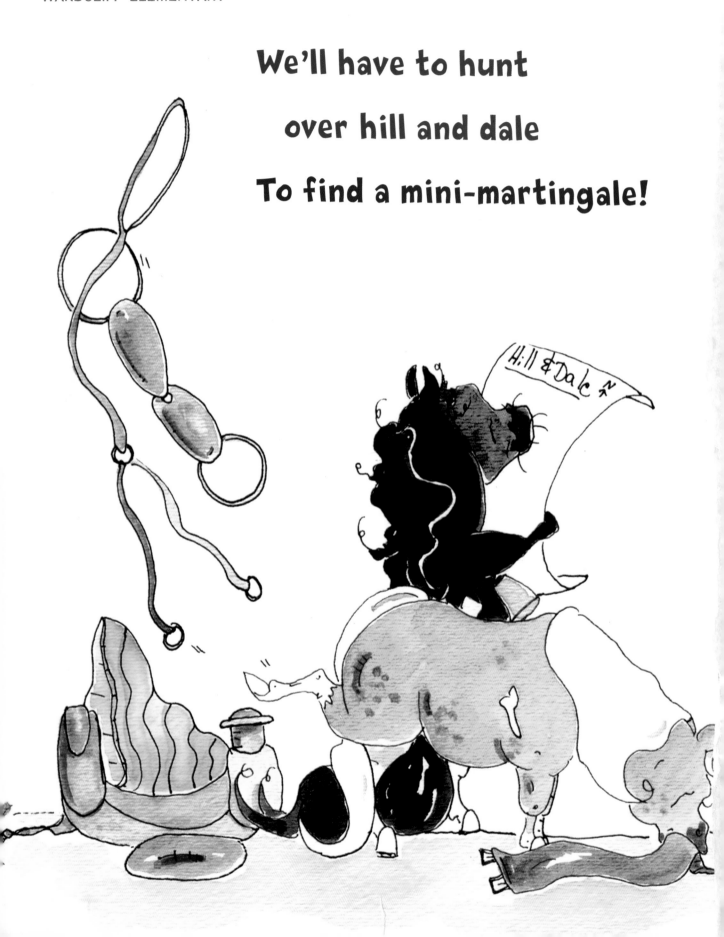